A WOODLAND MYSTERY

The Butterfly Farm Burglar

A WOODLAND MYSTERY
By Irene Schultz

Mc Graw Hill **Wright Group McGraw-Hill**

To my daughter-in-law Lee Olivier, far away
but close to my heart

The Butterfly Farm Burglar
Copyright ©2000 Wright Group/McGraw-Hill
Text by Irene Schultz
Cover illustrations by Meg Aubrey
Cameo illustrations by Taylor Bruce
Interior illustrations by Cheryl Kirk Knoll and Adam Weiskind

Woodland Mysteries® is a registered trademark of
Wright Group/McGraw-Hill.

Wright Group/McGraw-Hill
19201 120th Avenue NE, Suite 100
Bothell, WA 98011
www.WrightGroup.com

Printed in the United States of America

10 9 8 7 6 5 4 3 2

ISBN: 0-322-01961-3
ISBN: 0-322-02374-2 (6-pack)

What family solves mysteries ... has adventures all over the world ... and loves oatmeal cookies?

It's the Woodlanders!

Sammy Westburg (10 years old)
His sister Kathy Westburg (13)
His brother Bill Westburg (14)
His best friend Dave Briggs (16)
His best grown-up friend Mrs. Tandy
And Mop, their little dog!

The children all lost their parents, but with Mrs. Tandy have made their own family.

Why are they called the Woodlanders? Because they live in a big house in the Bluff Lake woods. On Woodland Street!

Together they find fun, mystery, and adventure. What are they up to now?

Read on!

Meet the Woodlanders!

Sammy Westburg
Sammy is a ten-year-old wonder! He's big for his fifth-grade class, and big-mouthed, too. He has wild hair and makes awful spider faces. Even so, you can't help liking him.

Bill Westburg
Bill, fourteen, is friendly and strong, and only one inch taller than his brother Sammy. He loves Sammy, but pokes him to make him be quiet! He's in junior high.

Kathy Westburg
Kathy, thirteen, is small, shy, and smart. She wants to be a doctor someday! She loves to be with Dave, and her brothers kid her about it. She's in junior high, too.

Dave Briggs

Dave, sixteen, is tall and blond. He can't walk, so he uses a wheelchair and drives a special car. He likes coaching high-school sports, solving mysteries, and reading. And Kathy!

Mrs. Tandy

Sometimes the kids call her Mrs. T. She's Becky Tandy, their tall, thin, caring friend. She's always ready for a new adventure, and for making cookies!

Mop

Mop is the family's little tan dog. Sometimes they have to leave him behind with friends. But he'd much rather be running after Sammy.

Table of Contents

Chapter 1:
Hundreds of Butterflies

A red van pulled to a stop in a parking lot in Scotland.

Three children jumped out.

Ten-year-old Sammy shouted, "Hooray! We finally got here!"

Bill, fourteen, grinned at his younger brother.

He said, "We had to come ... just so we could get a little peace and quiet!

"Sammy, you've been talking about this butterfly place non-stop for a year ... ever since you heard about it."

Kathy Westburg, thirteen, the boys' sister, opened the van's back door.

The three children lifted a wheelchair out.

Dave Briggs, sixteen, was waiting for it in the van.

They wheeled the chair to him. He lowered himself into it.

Mrs. Tandy, the fifth member of the Woodland family, stepped down from the driver's seat. It was on the right side in Scotland.

She said, "I really have to think about every move I make when I drive.

"It's all backward from how WE drive in the United States.

"Too bad they didn't have a hand-control van here, Dave. Then we could share the driving."

The family moved toward a big, plain-looking building.

Sammy was far ahead ... until he got a good look at the building. Then he stopped dead in his tracks.

He groaned, "Just a minute! This is IT? This is what we came all the way to Scotland to see?

"No wonder they didn't show the building on their folder.

"They just showed butterflies.

"The building's so ugly and plain, they probably only have ten butterflies.

"And those will probably be just a couple like the ones that fly around Edinburgh."

He said the name of the town like this: ED-in-burr-uh.

He frowned as he followed the others inside.

There they saw a room with books ... and a woman at a desk.

Dave wheeled up to the desk. He paid for five tickets.

Sammy whispered, "I knew it! Where are the butterflies?"

The woman pointed to a doorway. Long plastic strips hung from the top down to the floor.

She said, "The butterflies are right through there.

"Those plastic strips stop the butterflies from getting out."

Dave wheeled right through the strips into the next room.

A second later, he called, "Hey! Wow! Wait till you see this!"

4

He sounded so excited, the others hurried after him. And they saw ...

BUTTERFLIES! Butterflies everywhere!

Hundreds of beautiful butterflies filled the air. All sizes. All colors.

One landed on Kathy's head.

Another one touched down on Sammy's stomach.

5

Sammy pointed ahead ... to a big, round, stone table.

"LOOK!"

Ten HUGE, bright blue butterflies sat on the table.

Bill said, "Look, they're sucking on slices of oranges."

Dave said, "Jungle butterflies, right here in Edinburgh. And some of these trees and bushes look like jungle plants."

Sammy said, "The camera! Give me the camera, Bill! Quick!"

Bill laughed. "It's hanging around your neck, Sammy."

Sammy grabbed it. He snapped a picture of the stone table covered with blue butterflies.

Mrs. Tandy said, "My goodness! Look here. Quick!"

Sammy turned and saw that six butterflies had landed on her arms.

He snapped photos of her.

Bill said, "Hey, I hope we packed plenty of film!"

They started walking down separate paths.

There were trees and bushes growing everywhere.

After a few steps, they could hardly see each other.

Suddenly Sammy called out, "Everybody, come over this way! A bunch of little birds are running around here near me."

Dave wheeled over and said, "I think those are some kind of quail.

"What are they doing in a butterfly house?"

Just as David said that, something moved from behind a thick bush. It was a tall man on his knees. He was holding a digging tool.

7

He stood up and grinned.

His thick hair hung down in front to his eyebrows.

It made Kathy think of a pony's mane.

He had a long, strong face, a little like a pony's, too.

He had deep smile lines around his eyes and mouth.

He said, "I look after things here. I'm Kevin Dumfrey.

"That's DUM ... like too dumb to go home at the end of the day.

"And FREE ... like free to do what I like ... raise butterflies.

"And I LOVE it when people ask questions I can answer! It makes me feel so smart."

"Those birds ARE quail ... Chinese Painted Quail."

Sammy said, "How come they're in a butterfly place?"

Kevin Dumfrey said, "Some spiders and slugs kill plants. But we can't kill them with spray. Spray might kill our butterflies.

"Now, those quail LOVE to eat spiders and slugs. But they leave our butterflies alone.

"So they're our natural form of pest control."

Mrs. Tandy said, "Mr. Dumfrey, this is a wonderland!

"I can't believe anyone could make a place as beautiful as this."

Kevin Dumfrey smiled. He said, "Ma'am, that's music to my ears.

"Tell you what. Look around in this room as long as you want.

"When you're done, come into my back room. You won't BELIEVE what you'll see there."

Then he turned down a path and disappeared from sight.

Chapter 2:
The Caterpillar Killer

Bill said, "Let's finish looking at this room
fast.

"We can always come back.

11

"I want to see what Mr. Dumfrey's got in that other room."

Sammy said, "I know what Mrs. T's got ... a new BOYfriend!

"You heard him. She made music to his ears!"

Mrs. Tandy laughed and made a grab for Sammy's ear.

Sammy ducked away and giggled.

Kathy said, "Which path should we follow?"

Bill said, "Let's go to where I was when Sammy called us. There's a pond I want you to see.

"It has GREAT goldfish ... as long as your arm."

Sammy said, "Hey, I'm going to take notes!

"Maybe I'll even do a project about butterflies ... for my school science fair this year."

Bill said, "Well, just follow me. There are two stone benches at the pond. We can all sit there while you write."

They walked toward the benches, but they were disappointed.

A young worker was lying on one of them.

His shovel and pail and broom were on the other.

Kathy whispered, "There's no room for us."

Just then, something fell onto the man's arm. It was a yellow and black caterpillar.

The man jumped up.

Quick as a cat, he brushed the caterpillar off.

Then he lifted his foot and STAMPED on it!

Sammy ran right up to him.

He said, "Hey, why did you do that?

"You should be SAVING caterpillars, not killing them!

"That caterpillar wouldn't have hurt you!

"And it would have been a butterfly some day.

"And I could have studied it for my science project!

"I bet Kevin Dumfrey would be SO MAD if he saw you kill one of his caterpillars!"

The man frowned and said, "I stepped on it by mistake!"

Then he whispered so only Sammy

would hear, "Now, out of my way, you cheeky little rat, before I step on YOU."

He picked up his things and walked down the nearest path.

The others came up to Sammy.

Bill said, "We heard what that guy said ... that he stepped on it by mistake.

"Huh! That was no mistake!"

Mrs. Tandy said, "Why would a man like that be working here?"

Sammy said, "Well, anyway, the benches are empty now.

"Let me write a few things down. Then we can look around some more."

So they watched the butterflies flying around them.

After a while, Sammy said, "Hey, listen to this. It's a poem for the start of my project."

He read this:

"We saw a small quail,

With a very small tail.
The things that were yummy,
He put in his tummy.
Like spiders and slugs,
And quite a few bugs."
Dave said, "Hey, Sammy. I think that's very good.

"Except maybe you should say 'insects' instead of 'bugs.'"

Bill said, "That's right, Sammy. We studied them last year. Bugs are a certain KIND of insect ... with long noses for sucking.

"Looks like you'll have to change your poem."

Sammy said, "Sure, Bill.

"Sure, I'll change it ... as soon as you tell me a word that rhymes with 'insects'! Now keep YOUR long nose out of my poem!

"And bug off! My poem is PERFECT

16

the way it is.

"And right now I want to go see Kevin Dumfrey in the back room."

Kathy held out her hand and said, "Sammy, take a look at this caterpillar I just picked up from the floor."

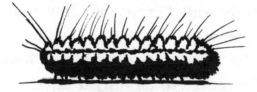

He took a long look. He touched its black and brown fur.

Then he said, "I love it. I want to stay here forever.

"In fact, I'm going to be a butterfly man like Kevin Dumfrey.

"And right now I'm going to ask him for a job. Come on!"

They followed a curving stone path

toward the back room. But something blocked the way.

It was the man who had killed the caterpillar.

He was sweeping the path, slowly, very slowly. He acted as if he didn't care how much time he wasted.

Dave said, "Excuse me, but may we get by, please?"

The man gave him a sour look.

He moved aside only a little. They had to inch past him.

Sammy whispered, "Now I KNOW Mr. Dumfrey will give me a job here some day!

"I'm a LOT nicer than THAT guy, without even trying!"

Sammy pushed through the plastic strips in the doorway.

Then they heard him exclaim, "WOW! I don't believe this!"

Chapter 3:
The Back Room

Bill said, "Come on. Let's see what's up!"

The Woodlanders pushed through the plastic strips.

Facing them were trees and bushes forming a small woods.

Crawling on them were HUNDREDS OF CATERPILLARS ... all different sizes ... all different colors ... hairy and smooth.

Some of them looked tiny and dry, like little twigs.

Some were big and fat, like little green hot dogs.

Then Kevin Dumfrey walked toward the Woodlanders.

On the back of his hand sat a giant insect!

It nearly hid his whole hand. It was light green.

It was long, and pointed at the back end.

Its sides were jagged like a saw blade.

Sammy took a closer look and pulled back.

Mrs. Tandy said, "Does that thing bite,

Mr. Dumfrey?"

Kevin Dumfrey laughed.

He said, "First of all, please call me Kevin.

"And no, this little lady won't hurt me.

"She's a Jungle Nymph." He said the word like this: NIMF.

"She can't sting, and she only eats leaves, not people.

"Say, maybe one of you would like to hold her?"

Sammy said, "Yuck!" and moved a step back.

But Kathy stepped forward and said, "I'd like to!"

Kevin said, "Hold out the back of your hand."

Kathy held out a shaking hand.

For a few seconds the insect stood perfectly still. Then it lifted its legs one at a time.

Slowly the nymph walked onto Kathy's hand.

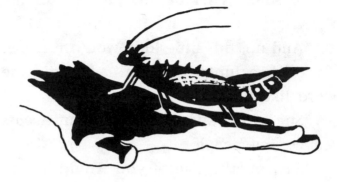

Sammy said, "GROSS!"

But Kathy said, "Why, it feels like a bird! Once you get used to it, it isn't scary at all."

Dave said, "I think I'd like to hold it, too, Kevin."

Mrs. Tandy said, "I'd like to give it a try."

Bill added, "Me, too ... if we won't be wearing it out."

That was too much for Sammy. He said, "Just a minute. I have dibs on holding it next."

Kevin said, "What does that mean, 'I have dibs'?"

Kathy said, "It means you get the first try at something."

Bill said, "When did you get dibs on it, Sammy?"

Sammy said, "Just now! When I said 'dibs.'"

Bill laughed and said, "OK, let Sammy do it next."

After him, they all took a turn.

Then Kevin led them to the other side of the room.

He put the nymph back in a glass case there.

He said, "I'll show you some of our other rare insects."

But Mrs. Tandy said, "Wait a minute!

What in the world is that?"

She was pointing above their heads, to a thick rope.

It was about nine feet in the air. It stretched across the whole room.

One end went into some bushes. The other end dipped down to a big pile of dirt.

Bits of pink and green stuff were moving all over it!

Bill said, "Wait a minute! That rope's ALIVE!"

Then he took a closer look.

It wasn't the rope that was alive. It was ants, thousands of ants, crawling along the rope.

Dave said, "Look at them. They're walking in both directions. And the ones coming toward us are carrying stuff in their mouths!"

Kevin pointed at the big pile of dirt.

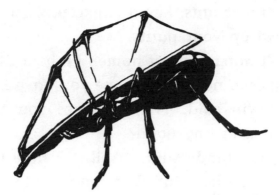

He said, "That's their home. They're leaf-cutter ants.

"We figured out just how far they'll go to get their food ... and we cut our rope that long.

"Then we planted bushes they like at one end of the rope.

"They bring their groceries home along the rope.

"Then they grow a certain kind of mold on bits of leaves, and eat it."

Sammy said, "That does it! Now I KNOW I want a job here.

"I love ants, Kevin ... except when they crawl up your pants.

"I watch ants at home. I'll be a GREAT helper ... not like the one you have now."

Kevin said, "What makes you think Matt isn't any good?"

Mrs. Tandy said, "Well ... I hate to be a tattletale. But that man really hates insects."

Kathy said, "We saw him push a caterpillar off his shoulder."

Dave said, "And then he stamped on it, on purpose."

Bill said, "And then he lied and said it was an accident."

Kevin said, "Thank heavens he's only here till the end of next week.

"I thought he might not be any good at it ... but I felt I HAD to give him a chance."

Dave said, "But what on earth for?"

Chapter 4:
Matt Makes Problems

Sammy said, "Why did you HAVE to hire that man?"

Kevin said, "Well, because of his grandfather.

"I'd do anything I could for his grandfather.

"Matt lives with him ... in a castle not far from here, and ... ."

Sammy said, "You're kidding! Is Matt's grandpa a king?"

Kevin said, "No, but he's a king of a person.

"Dan McDuff is an earl."

He said it like this: ERL.

"He's very rich, and he spends his money helping people.

"And he loves butterflies.

"Lots of times he comes and works here, just for fun.

"He even takes care of the jungle nymph and our tarantula."

Bill said, "But what has that got to do with hiring Matt?"

Kevin said, "Matt has become a real problem at home.

28

"He's been in trouble with the law several times.

"Dan McDuff asked me to take him on. Dan thought working here might change him."

Dave said, "Has it?"

Kevin said, "Hasn't seemed to help much.

"And he's made trouble here since the first day he rode up on his motorbike.

"We just haven't been able to count on him.

"You see, we buy cocoons and chrysalises from all over the world."

He said that word like this: KRIS-uh-liss-ez.

"We raise them in those glass cases over there."

He pointed to several cases set into the wall. Inside the cases, wooden sticks ran along the ceilings.

Hanging from the sticks were dozens of cocoons ... and golden-brown, hard-looking things.

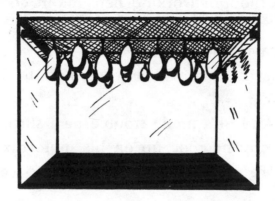

He pointed to those.

He said, "These are chrysalises. They will become butterflies.

"And inside each cocoon is a pupa."

He said the word like this: PYOO-puh.

"It will become a moth.

"We glue the cocoons and chrysalises to those sticks. Moths and butterflies hatch out of them, right before our eyes.

"We never lost track of a cocoon ... until Matt got here.

"Since he came, two rare cocoons from Japan have gotten lost. And we never found them."

Dave said, "Did he lose them gluing them to the sticks?"

Kevin said, "Well, maybe the first one. So I didn't let him help me hang the next bunch.

"I glued them up myself. Later I found that one was missing.

"Maybe he took a look at them and knocked one down by accident.

"Well, anyway, come take a look in this other cage.

"It's not an insect, but it's a cousin of the insects."

They stared through the glass. On the other side, a HUGE, hairy, orange and black SPIDER was staring back at them.

Sammy almost shouted, "IT'S A TARANTULA!"

He said the word like this: ter-AN-choo-luh.

Behind Kevin, a school class came in. The children heard Sammy.

"A tarantula!"

"Where is it?"

"Let me see it!"

The Woodlanders stepped back to let the class take a look.

Kevin led the family to another glass cage. This one was marked RHINOCEROS BEETLE.

He reached in. He lifted something out of it.

It was a black beetle as big as a pear!

Three sharp-looking horns stuck out of the front of its head.

Sammy said, "He looks like his horns could KILL you!"

Kevin said, "Don't worry. THIS rhinoceros beetle can't kill anybody ... he's dead.

"And he smells just AWFUL! Don't breathe near him.

"He died last month. We haven't gotten our new one in yet.

"I keep this one just to show off his wings."

Kathy said, "Wings! Where?"

Kevin said, "Folded right under this black shell."

He slowly lifted one side of the beetle's shell.

Then he spread open a huge, beautiful lacy wing from underneath.

Sammy ducked in close for a really good look.

Then he grabbed his nose. "Pee-yoo! I see how you knew it was dead! Let me out of here!"

Kathy laughed. She said, "It's time for us to go, anyway.

"The Princes Street Gardens are next. Remember?"

Mrs. Tandy said, "That's right. We'd better get going.

"I have my field glasses. We can even do some bird watching."

Sammy said, "I don't want to get out of here. I was just kidding."

Dave said, "Well, why don't we come back tomorrow?"

Just then, Matt stamped into the room. With a bang, he dropped a pail into the sink.

He pushed through the crowd and up to Kevin.

He said, "I forgot to tell you that I'm leaving early today.

"My grandfather told me to meet him at two o'clock."

Before Kevin could answer, Matt turned and left.

Sammy said, "Kevin, you won't have your helper anymore today.

"So I'll empty and wash out the pail.

"And I'll wash out the mop.

"And you'll see what a great helper I'll be some day.

"And no one will have to look at Matt's grouchy face ... for the rest of the day!"

But Sammy was so wrong!

Chapter 5:
Caught in a Lie

The Woodlanders' first stop was for sandwiches.

Sammy had his mouth full when he
began to talk.

A blob of chewed cheese sandwich fell on his T-shirt.

Calmly, he lifted up his shirtfront and licked the blob back into his mouth.

Bill said, "Gross! You've been wearing that shirt all morning! It's dirty."

Sammy said, "My science teacher says we all eat a bushel of dirt in our lives.

"This'll just make my bushel a little fuller."

They finished eating and drove to the Princes Street Gardens.

They followed a wide walk down into the park.

Sammy said, "Look at this place! It's bigger than a football field."

Dave said, "It could be bigger than ten football fields!"

The park was full of sweet-smelling flowers.

Seagulls flew overhead, calling across

the bright sky.

Kathy said, "No wonder everybody comes here.

"But it doesn't seem at all crowded ... except at those booths.

"I wonder what's going on."

Mrs. Tandy said, "I saw a sign as we came down. There's a craft show. Handmade sweaters and beads and such."

Sammy said, "I don't want to look at dumb old sweaters!

"Hey, where's that music coming from?

"It sounds like an elephant playing a big mouth organ. LOUD! Like it wants to be heard by the herd.

"Get it? Heard and herd! It's a joke."

Bill groaned.

Then Dave said, "Look, that's where it's coming from ... that stage with those men dancing on it. And there are bagpipe players."

Kathy said, "Look over there by those trees. There's a marching band putting on a show."

Mrs. Tandy said, "My, it's hard to decide what to do first."

Bill pointed to a puppet stage. He said, "Let's go there.

"It's an old-fashioned Punch-and-Judy show."

Sammy said, "Yeah, let's go to the puppet show first!

"Look, Judy's hitting an alligator over the head with a stick!

"And now the alligator has the stick. Now he's hitting Judy over the head."

Suddenly, Sammy stopped talking. He grabbed Bill's arm.

In a loud whisper, he said, "Forget the puppet show.

"Head for the craft show! Fast, everybody!"

They followed him to the nearest craft booth.

Sammy darted behind the wall of the booth. He smiled at the woman in charge.

He took down a blue and yellow sweater. He looked it over as if he might buy it.

Bill whispered, "Hey, what's up? You said that you didn't want to look at sweaters."

Sammy peeked around the wall toward the puppet show.

Bill poked him in the ribs. He said, "What are you up to?

"This is a ROTTEN way to watch the puppet show."

Sammy said, "Stop poking me! I'm not watching the puppet show.

"I'm watching MATT! Matt from the BUTTERFLY FARM!

"He's at that show! And he's talking to someone."

Bill said, "So? Everyone meets friends at the Princes Street Gardens. You heard him. He's meeting his grandfather."

Sammy said, "He is NOT! Not unless his grandfather is about seventeen with ...

pointy green hair

a safety pin for an earring

... and a blue tattoo.

"Take a look, Bill."

Mrs. Tandy said, "Let me see!"

Kathy said, "Me, too."

They all peeked out ... and ducked right back in.

Mrs. Tandy said, "Sammy's right. That sure isn't a grandpa."

Kathy said, "Maybe they're BOTH waiting for Matt's grandpa."

Sammy said, "Not on your life! They're not looking for ANYone."

Bill said, "I bet Matt was lying about meeting his grandfather ... so he could meet this green-haired boy today instead."

Dave said, "They have a big paper spread out on their laps."

Kathy took another peek.

She said, "The green-haired boy is pointing to stuff on it."

Dave said, "It looks to me like a big map. I wonder what they're so interested in?"

Sammy said, "Well, I know how we can find out.

"Mrs. Tandy, can Kathy use your field glasses?"

Mrs. Tandy said, "Of course. But what on earth for?"

Sammy said, "Here's what.

"Kathy's small and quiet. Matt probably never even noticed her back at the butterfly farm.

"Kathy, you go sit down on the last bench at the puppet show.

"Pretend you're looking at seagulls ... with the field glasses.

"But every once in a while, zero in on that map.

"Find out what it is. Will you do it?"

Chapter 6:
Sammy Disappears

Kathy said, "I hate to sneak around and spy.

"But then, why did Matt lie to Kevin about meeting this boy? Is it something that would hurt the butterfly farm?

"Give me the field glasses, Mrs. T. I'll do it."

She started walking slowly toward the puppet show.

Sammy hated doing nothing, so he looked at the blue and yellow sweater again.

He said, "Hey, look at this, Mrs. T. That's a cute-looking dog on the front ... it looks a lot like our dog at home.

"Except this one is yellow ... and Moppy is tan.

"You know, I think I really like this sweater."

Then he stopped talking to watch Kathy.

She didn't move fast, for fear Matt would notice her.

Finally, she sat down on the end of the last bench. It was eleven rows behind Matt and the green-haired boy.

She lifted the field glasses and aimed them at the sky.

Then she lowered them toward Matt and Green Hair.

She kept moving sideways until she was right in back of them.

Now the family was worried.

But Matt didn't look toward Kathy ... and after a moment, she walked back to the family.

Sammy hugged her.

He said, "Kathy, you're a GREAT snoop! What did you see?"

Kathy said, "Well, they're looking at a map, all right ... of a place called Arthur's Seat.

"The map shows the shape of different parts of the land, and how high they all are.

"It even shows the shapes of some of the rocks."

Dave said, "I've read about Arthur's Seat.

"The Edinburgh book said it's a huge, wild hill with paths all over it. It's long, and it's shaped a little like a loaf of bread.

"People from Edinburgh love to walk around on it.

"But only really good climbers try to climb the high, rocky part.

"Arthur's Seat was a volcano millions of years ago.

"So it's covered with rocks that boiled up out of it.

"I think that part is called the neck of the volcano."

Kathy said, "Well, the rocky part is what Matt's interested in.

"He kept asking questions about it. And the green-haired boy kept pointing to things on the map."

Mrs. Tandy said, "That's a surprise to me.

"Matt seems too lazy to be much of a mountain climber."

Bill said, "Come on, let's take a walk through the park. Matt doesn't have to spoil our afternoon."

Sammy said, "Wait a minute. I want to buy this sweater."

Bill said, "You called them 'dumb old sweaters.'"

Sammy said, "Well, YOU'D probably choose a dumb old sweater.

"But this blue one is great, and it's mine."

He paid for it and said, "I'll just wear it now. That wind's cold."

He put it on. He patted the yellow dog on the front.

He said, "OK, let's go look at those dancers."

■　■　■

The men danced in a group to the bagpipe music.

Then one of the dancers took over by himself.

He laid his sword on the stage, and his sword case across it.

He began a fast dance, moving his feet in and out around them.

Bill said, "Look at that! One wrong step and he cuts his foot!"

Sammy said, "Big deal! I could dance like that ... if I had a sword. Wait, I'll show you."

He ran over to some bushes. He fished around under them. He pulled out two dead branches.

He laid them across each other on the grass.

He began jumping around. Half the time he hit the branches.

Bill said, "You look like a bouncing ball that's gone nuts.

"Lucky you DIDN'T have a sword! We'd be calling a doctor."

Sammy stuck out his tongue.

He said, "I don't see YOU trying to do it, babycakes.

"You're afraid you'd hurt your little widdle toes!"

Then he dashed across the park toward the big marching band.

He turned to wave at Bill and stick out his tongue.

Then he disappeared behind the band.

Kathy said, "He could get lost."

Bill said, "Don't worry. If he doesn't show up, I'll go find him."

In a minute or two, Bill got worried himself.

He ran to the other side of the band.

He couldn't see Sammy. But in the distance he DID see some faces he knew.

Matt and Green Hair were sitting on a bench!

They had moved from the puppet show into the sunlight.

They were still looking at their big map.

Behind their new bench was a big stand of thick bushes.

Behind the bushes stood a gray stone wall.

Between the bushes and the wall, Bill could see something waving.

It was a bright blue and yellow flag!

Chapter 7:
Let's Go to Arthur's Seat

It wasn't a flag. It was Sammy's new sweater!

Sammy was behind the bushes, against the wall.

And Bill figured Sammy wanted HIM back there, too.

So first, Bill walked way over to the right.

Then he walked toward the gray stone wall.

Then he moved left along the wall. He reached the bushes and slipped behind them.

He got down to crawl between them and the wall.

He had to move slowly. He didn't want to snap any dead branches and make noise.

Finally, he reached Sammy.

Sammy signaled with his hand, "Follow me."

The two boys crawled nearer, behind Matt's bench.

They could hear the heavy map being moved about.

Matt and Green Hair were still looking at it.

Matt was asking questions: "How high
is this spot? And how about there? Can
it be seen easily from below?

"Which spot is the farthest from where
most people walk?

"How long does it take to get there
from the parking area?"

Green Hair said, "These large stones,
right here, are on the highest part.

"I don't think you could get up there."

Matt said, "Is that a place where hardly anybody goes? That's what I'm looking for. That's what I'm paying you to
show me."

Green Hair said, "I guess so. But it's
very tricky.

"I've climbed up there only a couple
of times myself."

Matt said, "What's so tricky about it?

Just because it's high, that doesn't make it tricky."

Green Hair said, "The rocks are big, with sharp edges. They're very hard to climb up onto. And there are a lot of them.

"You could easily break a leg up there ... and no one would be around to get you down."

Matt asked, "Are there lots of spaces between the rocks?"

Green Hair said, "Sure, plenty of them. Between and under. Almost like little caves.

"But why would you ask that?"

Matt said, "I'm not paying you to ask questions. I ask the questions. I'm paying for answers.

"And you better remember ... watch for me in the parking lot nearest the top, tomorrow at two o'clock. I'll be on my motorbike.

"Now point out some other ways down from the rocky part.

"Are there footpaths along the front and sides of the rocks? All the way down to the bottom?

"Are they steep? Are they easy to follow?"

Bill had heard enough. He signaled to Sammy to follow him.

The boys crawled quietly back to the wall.

They crawled along it to the right, out of the bushes.

Then they signaled to the other Wood-landers to join them.

Bill said, "Sammy and I have something to tell you. We need to make new plans."

■   ■   ■

Sammy started talking the minute everyone got into the van. "Matt's going to Arthur's Seat tomorrow afternoon at two o'clock ...

"and Green Hair, too ...

"they're going to explore ...

"and what Matt is up to ...

"... is, um, um—"

Dave broke in. "Whoa, Sammy. Tell us everything ... slowly."

Sammy and Bill told them what they had done.

Mrs. Tandy said, "Talk about snoop-ing! You take the cake!

"My goodness, I wonder what Matt's

62

going to do?"

Kathy said, "Why don't we find out? We could go to Arthur's Seat tomorrow."

Dave said, "We would have to get there before two o'clock."

Sammy said, "Let's go at lunch time. We could have a picnic."

Mrs. Tandy said, "We should take warm clothes. And a blanket. It could get really cold.

"Edinburgh's weather changes all the time. They say it's summer, fall, winter, and spring every day."

Dave said, "OK, then, how does this sound?

"In the morning, we put warm clothes and food into the van.

"First, we go to the butterfly farm as we planned.

"At noon we drive over to Arthur's Seat.

"We find a place where no one will notice us."

Sammy said, "Then the Woodland spies have their picnic."

Bill said, "And when Matt arrives, we find out what he's up to."

Sammy said, "It's a perfect plan! It's got everything. Butterflies! Hiding! Snooping! Food!

"I can't wait until tomorrow!"

Chapter 8:
Up on Arthur's Seat

It was Thursday morning. The butterfly farm had just opened.

The Woodlanders walked in and saw Kevin.

Sammy was exploding with news.

The moment he saw Kevin, he blurted out, "HELLO, KEVIN, WE HAVE TO TALK TO YOU RIGHT AWAY. IS MATT HERE YET?"

Kevin said, "No. He's usually last to come in."

Dave said, "Good, because we have a lot to tell you.

"Yesterday afternoon, at the gardens, we saw Matt.

"He wasn't meeting his grandfather at all."

Bill said, "And I bet he comes up with the same story today ... that he has to meet his grandfather."

They told Kevin everything they knew.

And they told him their plans for Arthur's Seat.

Then they heard a motorbike pull up outside.

Matt walked in.

He frowned at them all and walked into the back room.

Sammy said, "If he were an insect, he'd be a stinkbug."

Bill said, "If he were a plant, he'd be a skunk cabbage."

Kathy said, "If he were a tree, he'd be a slippery elm."

Just then, a busload of visitors arrived.

Kevin took everyone outside to his beehives. He told them about raising bees. He gave them honeycomb to chew.

Sammy chewed most of his ... until suddenly he yelled, "Yuck!

"There's a bee in my piece! And I almost ate it!"

Kevin broke the bee off for him, and Sammy decided to eat the rest.

They washed their hands at the big sink under the cocoon case.

Suddenly, they heard Kevin exclaim, "No, not AGAIN!

"There's an empty spot on a stick. Another cocoon is missing!

"Where's Matt? He was supposed to keep an eye on things!"

But Matt was gone. A note on Kevin's desk said,

Kevin said, "This is the last straw! I hate to disappoint his grandfather, but Matt has to go.

"I'll want to hear what you find out about him today.

"So if you can trust my cooking, meet me at my place tonight for dinner."

They said they'd love to, and wrote down his address.

Dave followed the rest of the family out to the van.

On the way, he slowed his chair. He leaned over and picked up something from the ground.

■　■　■

Arthur's Seat was a HUGE rise of land.

It looked like the worn-down mountain that it was.

The family drove up the long road that wound up around it.

69

At last they came to a large space marked CAR PARK.

Sammy was wearing warm clothes.

He jumped out of the van. Then he jumped back in.

He said, "It's hot as a stove out there! I was sweating as soon as I stepped outside."

He took off his jacket.

He took off his new sweater.

He took off his scarf. He noticed a string of wool hanging from it.

So he used that to tickle Bill on the neck.

Bill thought it was a bug. He slapped himself on his neck, HARD.

Sammy laughed, LOUD.

He said, "Ha! I got you again with my old bug trick!"

Bill said, "You sound like a laughing hyena!

"What makes you think pestering me is so funny?"

That made Sammy laugh so hard, he rolled off the van seat.

Then Bill was laughing himself as he climbed out of the van.

Dave got into his wheelchair. He took out their box of picnic food.

He said, "Let's eat in that meadow, to the right."

To the left lay a meadow that was even bigger.

It rose up and up ... to a huge pile of gray rocks at its top.

Bill said, "I like this lower meadow. It's perfect for our picnic.

"We can see everyone who climbs toward the rocks.

"But a climber would have to turn to see us. And anyway, the grass would hide us."

They laid out the blanket and sat on it.

The wild grasses stood up around them like a wall.

Sammy had made his favorite sandwiches ... peanut butter, grape jelly, and dill pickles.

He took a big bite and said, "Say, why do they call this place 'Arthur's Seat,' anyway?"

Bill said, "Sammy, you pig, don't talk with your mouth full!

"It looks like the inside of a garbage truck!"

Sammy said, "Then don't look!" But he closed his mouth.

Mrs. Tandy said, "That's a good question, though, Sammy. Why IS this place called 'Arthur's Seat'?

"Maybe because it's shaped like a seat to sit on ... like a couch."

Bill said, "Or maybe it was a government center once, the seat of a kingdom."

Sammy said, "I'll tell you how they named it!

"It's because a guy named ARTHUR used to SIT up there. Don't you guys know anything?"

Then Sammy laughed and rolled over on top of Bill.

Bill pushed him off.

They were wrestling on the grass when Dave said, "Hold it, guys!

"You'll never guess who's walking across the big meadow, toward the rocks!"

Chapter 9:
Up to the Rocks

They looked toward the big meadow.

They saw the green-haired boy, with Matt following him.

The two of them were walking toward the high rocks.

A cloud passed over the sun. The wind began to blow hard.

Sammy said, "Hey, I felt some rain. And it's turned cold again. Wait a second. I'm putting my new sweater back on."

Dave said, "I won't be going up with you.

"That meadow is all up hill ... and the rain will make it slippery.

"It would be too hard to get my chair all the way up there."

Kathy said, "Then I'm staying down here with Dave."

Sammy said, "Come on, Kathy. Dave can live without his girl friend for a LITTLE while."

Bill poked Sammy. Mrs. Tandy grinned. Kathy turned pink.

Dave said, "Don't worry about me. I have something to do.

"And I'll watch you from the van, with the field glasses.

"Leave the picnic stuff. I'll clean up. See you later."

Matt and the green-haired boy were walking very fast.

So the Woodlanders began to hurry after them. The wet grass kept slapping against them.

After a while, Sammy said, "I bet we've walked for ten minutes. But we aren't even a third of the way up to those rocks.

"My pants are soggy.

"They're so heavy, they're almost falling down.

"And my legs are freezing. And my shoes are soaked.

"And I'm beginning to slip around in the mud.

"It's like walking in a mud-bottomed lake."

The rain was falling in fine drops. It formed a mist.

They had trouble seeing more than a few feet ahead.

People climbing the hill in front of them gave up ... turned around ... and started walking down.

Mrs. Tandy said, "What will we do if Matt gets tired of climbing?

"If he turns around, he might see us."

Sammy made his most terrible bulldog face.

He said, "Don't worry, Mrs. T. I'll save us."

He punched wildly as if he were fighting someone.

Bill laughed. "Come on, Sammy. What could Matt do to us?

"In this rain, he probably wouldn't even know who we are.

"And if he did, he'd think we came here today just by chance."

Now the climb got even harder and more uphill.

Sammy began huffing and puffing. He said, "This is a steep climb, right after lunch.

"Do you think Matt's going all the way up, onto those rocks?"

Kathy said, "If he does, do you think we should all go after him? He'd be sure to notice FOUR people."

Bill said, "I wish Dave were here to help decide."

After a while, Mrs. Tandy was a little out of breath.

She said, "I'm surprised to see Matt work so hard to get up this hill.

"He was so lazy at the butterfly farm, he hardly moved.

"NOW look! He's pulling himself up onto those huge rocks!"

Bill said, "We'd probably better stay below the rocks. We don't want him to notice us."

But Sammy said, "Well, he won't notice just ONE person. ME. So good-bye, you guys."

Before they could say anything, Sammy was up on the rocks.

Then he stooped down and whispered, "There are a million rocks up here.

"Mostly I'll be able to jump from one to another.

"But where they're far apart, I'll climb down. And then I'll just climb up onto the next one."

Mrs. Tandy said, "Oh, Sammy. Those rocks are slippery from the rain. Promise us you'll be careful."

Sammy said, "I'll be very careful. And anyway, Kathy's here.

"She's going to be a doctor. She can patch me up."

And he began making his way across the rocks.

■　　■　　■

Dave couldn't see the family through the mist.

So to keep busy, he pulled two small things from his pocket.

They were what he'd found that morning on the ground at the butterfly farm.

One of the things was a large, brown cocoon.

It had been cut open and now it was empty.

The other thing was a tiny piece of rolled paper. It was rolled tightly. Dave slid it into the cocoon. It fit perfectly.

Then he took it out again and unrolled it. It seemed to be a computer-written note.

It said,

vkfgn vlfgn vfk vkvgn vkfxg .kbng vkvd

"WHAT? It'll take time to figure this out," he thought.

82

So he decided to check back on what the family was doing instead.

He put the paper and the cocoon back into his pocket.

He picked up the field glasses and took a look up the meadow.

The rain was letting up. The mist had cleared.

He could see Kathy, Mrs. Tandy, and Bill standing in the grass.

Sammy was up on the rocks, hurrying back toward them.

He was waving his arms and leaping from stone to stone.

Dave thought, "He looks like a kangaroo gone bonkers! What's happened?"

Chapter 10:
Dinner and Detective Work

Mrs. Tandy watched Sammy jumping over the rocks.

She was thinking, "I can't just stand here watching him.   It looks so dangerous!"

But Sammy jumped back safely to a rock just above Bill.

Bill was so glad to see him, he half-lifted Sammy down.

Sammy said, "I don't need any help," but his voice sounded weak ... and he looked wild-eyed.

Mrs. Tandy asked, "What's wrong, honey? What happened? Are you OK?"

Sammy said, "Matt took a nose dive! Right off the rocks!

"Up there at the front edge.

"He was moving fast and he fell right over, head first!

"I was going to climb down and help him.

"But Green Hair was with him ... and I heard Matt talking. So I figured he wasn't hurt too badly."

Kathy asked, "Could you tell what he was doing up there?"

Sammy said, "No. All I know is, he climbed everywhere.

"He lay down and looked between rocks.

"And a couple of times, he climbed down between them.

"It looked like he was searching for something."

Bill said, "Well, let's get back and get cleaned up.

"Don't you remember? It's Kevin's place tonight for dinner."

Sammy said, "Oh, that's right! Hurry, everybody!"

Then he started singing, "Mrs. Tandy has a new BOYfriend, Mrs. Tandy has a new ... ."

Mrs. Tandy grabbed him ... and hugged him. She said, "I'm so glad YOU didn't take a nosedive ... I can't even get mad at you."

■ ■ ■

They got to the van and told Dave what they'd seen.

Dave showed them the cocoon and the little piece of paper.

He said, "I found them on the ground at the butterfly farm. I figure the paper was INSIDE the cocoon.

"And look what's written on the paper."

He unrolled it and showed them:

vkfgn vlfgn vfk vkvgn vkfxg .kbng vkvd

Kathy said, "That doesn't make sense. It must be some sort of code."

Bill said, "I just read about a GREAT code ... used in World War II. Turned out it wasn't a code at all, but a language.

"Two Navajo Indians sent messages in Navajo back and forth."

He said it like this: NAV-uh-hoe.

"Maybe those are Scottish words that we don't know."

Dave said, "I don't think so, but let's work on it later.

"Right now, let's get back to our hotel and get you into warm clothes."

■   ■   ■

A while later, they drove to Kevin's house.

Dave asked, "Kevin, may I take a look at your computer before we have dinner?"

Kevin showed Dave into his office. Then the others helped Kevin carry food to the table.

There was cold roast beef ...

salad

home-made bread

buttered carrots

honey

sugar

cream

... and a pot of tea.

Before they'd finished setting the table, Dave joined them.

Kevin carried in the last dish. It had something steaming-hot on it. It was light brown and shaped like a sagging balloon.

Kevin said, "My mother made this haggis for us."

He said it like this: HAG-iss.

"Have you ever tasted it? Haggis is Scotland's most famous dish."

Sammy said, "It looks like a fat, messy sausage."

He spooned some onto his plate. The others helped themselves and started in.

Sammy took a bite first. Then he munched some more.

He cleared the haggis off his plate in two big swallows.

He said, "Hey! I love this!"

Mrs. Tandy said, "It's SO good! How DO you make it?"

Kevin said, "Well, you chop up oatmeal and fat. You put in some chopped onions.

"Then you chop up a sheep heart. And the liver."

Sammy said, "Yuck!"

Kevin went on. "You chop up other

sheep parts, too ... all the parts that are too small to make into anything else.

"And you stuff all that into a sheep's stomach.

"And then you . . ."

Sammy grabbed his own stomach.

"THAT'S what I ate? A sheep's stomach stuffed with junk?

"GROSS!

"But I'll tell you what ... pass the haggis. Just don't tell us any more about it!"

Kevin laughed and passed the plate to Sammy.

Then he said, "Anyway, I have something better to talk about.

"Matt came in this afternoon ... and he asked to be paid. He had a bandage on his head.

"He said he'd tripped and hit it on the bathtub.

"He said he had already cleared out his locker."

At that moment, they heard the front door open.

A woman's voice called, "Kevin, I'm here!

"And wait until you see what's in the newspaper!"

Chapter 11:
Wonderful Paintings,
GONE!

An older woman walked into the dining room.

She looked a lot like Kevin, but not so tall.

She smiled and said, "Hello there. I'm Mrs. Dumfrey, Kevin's mother.

"Excuse me for a moment, Kevin. I have something to show you."

She handed a newspaper to her son.

For a few seconds, Kevin looked at the paper.

Then he said, "Oh my. Poor Dan McDuff."

Sammy said, "What's happened to him?"

Kevin said, "He's OK. But his castle has been robbed.

"It's full of wonderful paintings ... the kind you see in museums.

"The paper says four of them have been stolen. A painting by Turner. And one by Goya. And a Whistler. And a Hals.

"They were taken from a back bedroom of the castle.

"Some one took them ... and put full-size photos of the pictures into their frames instead."

Dave said, "A photo would look almost real."

Kathy said, "Yes, until the light hit it a certain way. Then it would look too smooth and flat."

Mrs. Dumfrey said, "This morning, Dan McDuff went to get a book from that bedroom.

"He noticed that the pictures looked different."

Sammy said, "Well, if you ask me ... the police should march right up to Matt and arrest him!

"I bet Matt would steal ANYthing in a second.

"He's a sneak.

"And that guy with the green hair probably helped him."

Kevin laughed. He said, "It would be easy to believe you were right, Sammy. Except for one thing.

"As soon as the loss was discovered, the detectives questioned everyone in the castle. And they searched the castle.

"What did they find? Nothing. Not one clue.

"So Matt is in the clear ... for now.

"The paintings are gone. And the thief isn't known."

Dave said, "Well look, everyone. It's way past midnight. We had better be on our way."

Sammy said, "I'll see you in the morning, Kevin, and I'll give you a hand."

Kevin said, "That will be wonderful. Maybe there will be some news about the missing pictures by then."

■　■　■

Several hours later, Dave was awakened by a loud whisper.

Bill was saying, "Stop that, Sammy! I'm trying to sleep! Let go of my nose, you pest."

Sammy whispered, "How did you know it was me?"

Bill whispered back, "Who else would grab my nose in the middle of the night?"

Sammy said, "I keep thinking about the paintings. I can't sleep."

Dave said, "Oh boy, am I glad you woke me. I was just going to wake everybody, and I fell asleep!

"Come on, we have to go somewhere! I only hope we aren't too late."

He pulled himself into his wheelchair. He grabbed a sheet of paper from beside his bed.

Sammy said, "Where are we going?"

Just then, Kathy and Mrs. Tandy rushed into the room.

Kathy said, "We can't sleep. We think Sammy was right.

"We think Matt stole the paintings and hid them somewhere."

Dave said, "That's what I think, too. And I think he hid them in the rocks. Yesterday!

"So go get dressed. Wear warm clothes in case we have a long wait."

Then they piled into the van and sped through the night toward Arthur's Seat.

Chapter 12:
Carjacked!

They drove to the back of the parking lot at Arthur's Seat.

Mrs. Tandy turned off the van's lights.

Dave turned on a little penlight. He showed them the sheet of paper he had brought.

He said, "On the way to Kevin's, I had a sudden idea.

"So I copied his computer keyboard before dinner.

"And last night after we were in bed, I worked out the code.

"I was going to show it to you then ... but I fell asleep!"

Here's what was on Dave's paper:

Q W E R T Y U I O P

A S D F G H J K L ;

Z X C V B N M , . /

Dave had written this below the keyboard letters:

vkfgn vlfgn vfk vkvgn vkfxg .kbng

firth forth fri fifth first light

He said, "Look.   Here's how the code works.

"You type your message.   But you rest your fingers on the wrong row of keys ... a row below where they should be.

"Now see those words, 'firth, forth,' and so on?

"That's what comes up if you read each letter one row higher."

Sammy said, "But the NEW message doesn't make sense, either!

"All those firths and forths and fifths and firsts and stuff."

Kathy said, "Well, wait a minute, Sammy. Part of it does.

"I think I know what 'firth forth' might mean.

"The Firth of Forth is where the River Forth flows into the sea. It's on our map."

Bill said, "And 'Fri' and 'fifth' might mean Friday the fifth.

"Today is Friday, and it's the fifth day of the month."

Mrs. Tandy said, "And 'first light' probably means dawn."

Dave said, "But does anyone know what 'fife' might mean? The only fife I know about is a little flute called a fife."

Bill said, "I know. The land on the north side of the Firth of Forth is called Fife."

Dave said, "Then that's it! Someone mailed messages to Matt inside the cocoons.

"That's why some cocoons were missing. Matt took them ... to get to the messages hidden inside.

"This message was in the cocoon that disappeared yesterday.

"That person might be telling Matt about meeting places.

"And this is where he wants to meet Matt ... to buy the stolen paintings. On the Fife side of the Firth of Forth, at first light on Friday the fifth."

Bill said, "Then we've got to get up onto those rocks FAST! Matt will come to get the paintings before the night is over."

Kathy said, "Well, this time for sure I'm staying in the van with Dave."

Bill said, "Lock the doors when we leave."

So Bill, Mrs. Tandy, and Sammy started up the hill.

Twenty minutes went by.

Kathy and Dave heard a faraway motor.

The noise grew louder.

Then a motorbike with its lights off drove right up to their van.

SMASH! The back window was broken. The van door swung open, and Matt climbed in!

He dragged his motorbike in with him.

He said, "All right, you two. Listen carefully.

"I've seen you and your pals. I figure you're trailing me.

"You two are going for a short ride with me now. And if you don't want your pals hurt, then don't try anything funny."

"Now, you can't move your legs," he said, pointing to Dave, "so you can't drive.

"And girlie, you're too young to know how."

"By the time you walk and get help, I'll be long gone.

"Just don't make any trouble, and your friends will be all right."

Dave said, "Better do just what he says, Kathy."

Then Matt got into the driver's seat. He drove down from Arthur's Seat and out of the city.

In ten minutes, they were bumping along a hilly country road.

Matt parked the van. He pulled his motorbike out.

He said, "Good-night, fools," and he rode off.

Kathy said, "We HAVE to get back ... but we can't!

"If only this van had hand controls so you could drive it, Dave!

"Or if only I could ... ."

Dave said, "Wait a minute, Kathy. Slow down. We CAN drive back. And we WILL!"

He leaned to the right, the driver's side.

He took hold of the steering wheel. Then he pulled his body sideways into the driver's seat.

Then he said, "Kathy, move right up

next to me.

"Sit way over here so that your legs can reach the pedals.

"This isn't safe, but we really have no choice.

"We have to get help to the family.

"You don't know how to steer, but I do.

"And I can't work the pedals, but you can.

"And you know which is the gas pedal, and which is the brake pedal.

"So between us, we can drive ... if we don't lose our nerve."

Kathy said, "But Dave, how will I know when to step on the gas ... and when to step on the brakes?"

Dave said, "I'll say 'gas' ... and you step on the gas, just a little.

"I'll say 'faster,' and you step on it harder.

"I'll say 'slower,' and you lighten up on it.

"I'll say 'brakes' and you bring us to a stop. I know we can do it."

He turned on the key and said, "Gas, Kathy."

Chapter 13:
The Capture

First, they backed up onto a grassy field to turn around.

For a second the van hardly moved.

Then it shot backward. Kathy jammed on the brakes.

The van jerked to a stop.

Kathy said, "I guess I hit the pedals too hard.

"Did I ruin anything?"

Dave said, "The van's OK. A little bumping won't hurt it."

Kathy tried again.

Ten tries later, they were driving almost like one person ... although slowly.

At last, they reached the road up to Arthur's Seat.

Suddenly, Kathy jammed on the brakes. The van's headlights had caught Matt speeding down the hill toward them on his motorbike!

They saw the bike skid and land on the side of the road.

Matt jumped away from it.

He raced into the bushes, like an animal running in the dark.

Kathy pointed. She said, "Hey, I just

saw someone running after Matt!

"In fact, I think it was two people. And in the rear-view mirror I saw someone with a flashlight ... running UP the road behind us."

Dave said, "We can't stop. We have to drive up and make sure the family's safe."

Kathy said, "But look there!"

She was pointing ahead. Sammy and Bill and Mrs. T. were all coming down the road!

■   ■   ■

Sammy was grinning like a jack-o'-lantern.

Bill and Mrs. Tandy were smiling the same way.

They climbed into the van and everyone began talking.

Kathy asked, "Who were those people chasing Matt?"

Sammy grinned and said, "The police."

Dave said, "But where did THEY come from?"

Sammy grinned a BIGGER grin. "They came from ME!

"I called Kevin before I left our hotel room.

"And I told him that we were coming up here.

"But I didn't tell you guys because you might think I was scared.

"Kevin called the police ... and they got

114

here right away ... and they climbed up the rocks ... and we were climbing down to look for you ... and ... ."

Sammy stopped to take a breath and Bill went on. "The police officers shined their flashlights up at us," he said.

"Mrs. T and I almost jumped out of our SKINS!

"But Sammy told us about calling Kevin.

"So we all climbed down off the rocks, because we knew it was the police.

"But then we didn't know what had happened to you, so we figured we should wait ... because Matt would be coming back."

Kathy said, "And the paintings?"

Sammy had caught his breath and was ready to talk. "Well, there we were, waiting near the rocks ... whispering to each other.

115

"It was pitch dark. It felt like Halloween night.

"And Bill was freezing to death. So we both squeezed into my new sweater. It's a lot bigger now."

Bill said, "We told the police about the cocoon and paper ... and how Dave worked out the code ... and what we think it means."

Mrs. Tandy said, "They told us that a small boat had been reported missing yesterday ... from the Fife side of the Firth of Forth.

"They think it was stolen to carry the paintings away.

"They're searching for it along the coast."

Sammy said, "And then Matt came. He was ALONE!

"He didn't have anyone with him. He was working alone.

"The green-haired boy wasn't in on it at all! It turns out he's just a guy who makes his living leading people on climbs around Arthur's Seat.

"Well, Matt climbed past us without seeing us.

"Then he climbed down with some packages.

"He didn't try going down the front part of the rocks.

"I guess he didn't want to fall on his head again."

Bill said, "When the police called 'STOP!' he threw the packages in every direction.

"We figured they were the paintings. We were afraid they'd get wet, or stepped on, or lost.

"So we ran to look for them.

"And that's when Matt jumped on his motorbike and rode off."

Sammy said, "But we knew the other officers down below would be able to catch him.

"And guess what? While we were waiting, the police officers invited us to visit their station!

"So maybe I'll be a detective in Scotland instead of a butterfly scientist."

"Oh, and there's one more thing ... the police officers let me call Kevin on their phone. And he invited us to come over for breakfast.

"He's warming up some more haggis for us. And his mom's making oatmeal scones.

"And he said he's got a big bottle of honey for the scones.

"He said he gets honey free from the farm bees."

Sammy licked his lips. Then he said, "Free HONEY? Well, good-bye detective work. I think I'm a butterfly man after all."

Then the Woodlanders piled into the van and set off for breakfast with their new friend Kevin.